MW01165034

Smithsonian Prehistoric Zone

Pteranodon

by Gerry Bailey
Illustrated by Karen Carr

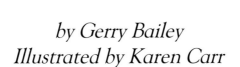

Crabtree Publishing Company

www.crabtreebooks.com

Crabtree Publishing Company

www.crabtreebooks.com

Author
Gerry Bailey

Illustrator
Karen Carr

Editorial coordinator
Kathy Middleton

Editor
Lynn Peppas

Proofreader
Kathy Middleton

Prepress technician
Samara Parent

Print and production coordinator
Katherine Berti

Library of Congress Cataloging-in-Publication Data

Bailey, Gerry.
   Pteranodon / by Gerry Bailey ; illustrated by Karen Carr.
      p. cm. -- (Smithsonian prehistoric zone)
   Includes index.
   ISBN 978-0-7787-1813-0 (pbk. : alk. paper) -- ISBN 978-0-7787-1800-0
(reinforced library binding : alk. paper) -- ISBN 978-1-4271-9704-7
(electronic (pdf))
   1. Pteranodon--Juvenile literature. I. Carr, Karen, 1960- ill. II. Title. III.
Series.

   QE862.P7B34 2011
   567.918--dc22

                                          2010044030

Library and Archives Canada Cataloguing in Publication

Bailey, Gerry
   Pterandon / by Gerry Bailey ; illustrated by Karen Carr.

(Smithsonian prehistoric zone)
Includes index.
At head of title: Smithsonian Institution.
Issued also in electronic format.
ISBN 978-0-7787-1800-0 (bound).--ISBN 978-0-7787-1813-0 (pbk.)

   1. Pteranodon--Juvenile literature. I. Carr, Karen, 1960-
II. Smithsonian Institution III. Title. IV. Series: Bailey, Gerry.
Smithsonian prehistoric zone.

QE862.P7B33 2011   j567.918   C2010-906888-2

Crabtree Publishing Company

Published in the United States
Crabtree Publishing
PMB 59051
350 Fifth Avenue, 59th Floor
New York, New York 10118

Published in Canada
Crabtree Publishing
616 Welland Ave.
St. Catharines, Ontario
L2M 5V6

Printed in China/012011/GW20101014

Dinosaurs

Living things had been around for billions of years before dinosaurs came along. Animal life on Earth started with single-cell **organisms** that lived in the seas. About 380 million years ago, some animals came out of the sea and on to the land. These were the ancestors that would become the mighty dinosaurs.

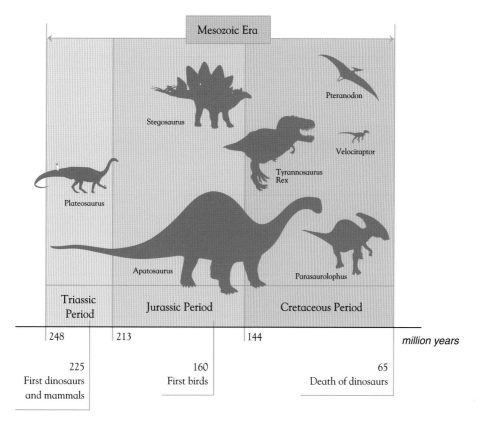

The dinosaur era is called the Mesozoic era. It is divided into three parts called the Triassic, Jurassic, and Cretaceous periods. Flowering plants grew for the first time during the Cretaceous period. Plant-eating dinosaurs, such as *Parasaurolophus*, roamed the land. Meat-eaters, such as *Tyrannosaurus rex* and *Velociraptor*, fed on the plant-eaters and other dinosaurs. Marine reptiles, such as *Tylosaurus*, swam in the seas. *Pteranodon* flew during the Cretaceous period. By the end of the Cretaceous period, dinosaurs (except birds) had been wiped out. No one is sure exactly why.

Pteranodon spread her wings so that their great 23-foot (7-meter) span cast a shadow on the rocks. Then she leaped from the cliff and soared gracefully into the air.

Below her, a pack of slow-moving
dinosaurs made their way along a path.
She took no notice of them. They were
plant-eaters and so no threat to her.

Pteranodon's great wings carried her weight easily. Although her body seemed large it was made lighter by its hollow, thin-walled bones. She was able to flap her wings and was a good flyer. She could also spread them like sails and glide on air **currents**.

With the wind now behind her, Pteranodon
swooped down closer to the water. She
was hungry and needed something to eat.
She had large eyes and keen vision.

8

She could spot a school of fish moving just under the surface of the water. The great flying reptile ate **mollusks**, crabs, and insects. She liked fish the best because they gave her the most energy.

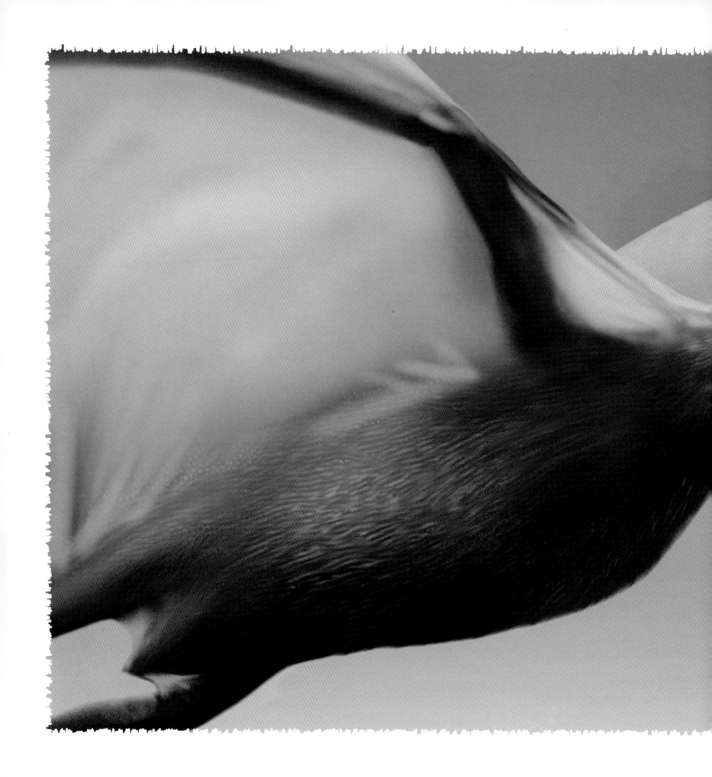

As she approached the surface of the
water, she opened her long beak. She
plunged it into the school of fish and
scooped up several silvery swimmers.

Pteranodon swallowed the fish
whole like a present-day pelican
would. She had no teeth to bite
or chew her food.

Pteranodon lowered her beak to scoop up more fish. She noticed the water below was gurgling and white with foam. She turned just in time to see a terrifying sea reptile called Tylosaurus.

Its huge jaws were open and ready to grab her. Tylosaurus was a **predator** that liked to feed on unsuspecting Pteranodons. And this one was hungry.

Pteranodon flapped her wings as hard as she could. She flew upward with her beak still full of fish. Tylosaurus snapped at her legs, but she was too quick.

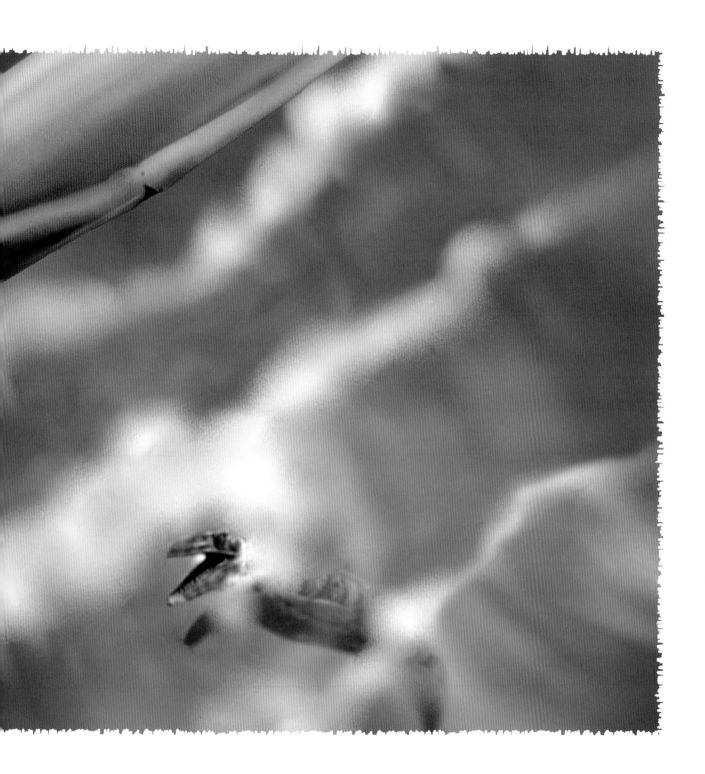

Her powerful wings carried her out of Tylosaurus's range. The frightening reptile opened its huge jaws and snapped again, but it could not reach Pteranodon. It would have to search for easier **prey**.

Pteranodon looked down at the angry Tylosaurus from high in the sky. She was a strong flyer and could stay in the air for a long time. She flapped her huge wings and flew off.

She looked down at a group of different flying reptiles from high above. It was a flock of pterosaurs, called Quetzalcoatlus, that were gliding far below her. Their long, **tapered** wings spread even wider than hers.

17

Pteranodon flew on past the flock of Quetzalcoatlus. She made her way farther out to sea. Then she saw another large school of fish. She dived down and scooped up a beak-full. But this time Pteranodon did not swallow them. She held them in her beak. She was going to take them back to her nest.

Pteranodon used a fast current of air to help her soar far up into the sky. She had drifted far out to sea and did not want to use too much energy flapping her wings.

She used different wind currents to dip down to the surface of the water and then up again. Pteranodon could glide like this for a long time without becoming tired. Sometimes she flapped her wings to gain speed.

As soon as she saw the cliff ahead of her, Pteranodon spotted her nest made of pine needles. She was greeted by the sound of small beaks opening and closing. They were eager to feed on the fish she had caught. Her young were growing quickly. Whenever Pteranodon returned they were ready to grab the food she carried in her beak.

The young Pteranodons greedily ate all the fish she had brought back. They were not satisfied. They needed a lot of food to help them grow and become strong. As soon as her beak was empty she had to fly off again in search of more fish. Very soon she would teach her young to fly so they would be able to hunt for themselves.

All about Pteranodon

(teh-RAN-uh-DON)

Pteranodon means "winged without teeth." It lived during the late Cretaceous Period around 89 to 80 million years ago. *Pteranodon* was among the largest of the flying reptiles to exist during this time. What made it such a capable flyer was its light weight. *Pteranodon's* bones were hollow and filled with air. Their walls were as thin as eggshells and they weighed very little. This kept *Pteranodon's* overall weight down. Its short tail helped as well. It would have made *Pteranodon* able to make quick turns and dives in the air.

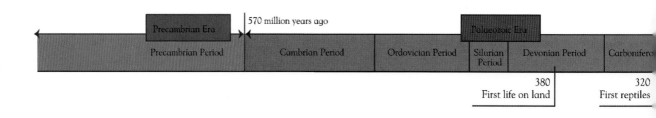

		570 million years ago					
Precambrian Era					Palaeozoic Era		
Precambrian Period		Cambrian Period	Ordovician Period	Silurian Period	Devonian Period		Carbonifero

380
First life on land

320
First reptiles

Unlike most other flying reptiles, *Pteranodon* had no teeth. Its beak was long and pointed. It may have used it to scoop up fish before swallowing them whole. It had sharp eyesight. This helped it find fish and insects, and maybe small land animals too. It had a large brain for its size, which would have made it a very good hunter.

Pteranodon's head could measure almost 7 feet (2 meters) and a large **crest** grew on the back of its head. No one knows for certain what the crest was used for. Some scientists believe it might have helped *Pteranodon* fly. It could have helped it balance in the air or steer and brake. Others believe it created an **aerodynamic** balance to its long head. The most likely explanation is that it was used for **display**. It was also most likely used to tell females apart from the males because the males had longer crests.

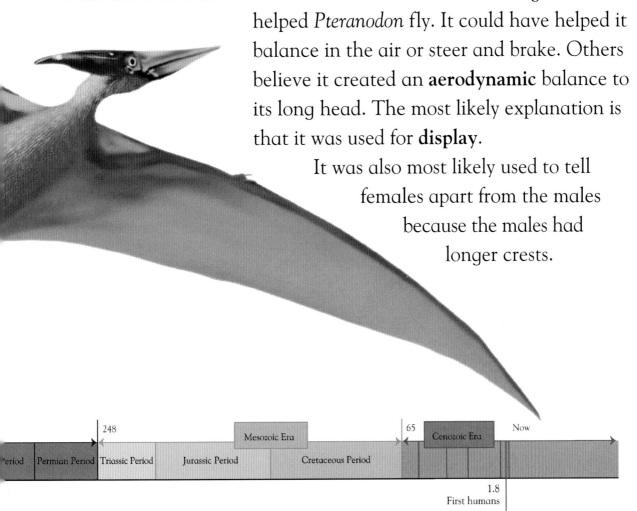

Period	Permian Period	Triassic Period	Jurassic Period	Cretaceous Period		Cenozoic Era	

248

Mesozoic Era

65

Cenozoic Era

Now

1.8
First humans

Flyer or glider?

Although *Pteranodon's* wingspan was huge, scientists are not sure how it used its wings. Some believe the *Pteranodon* was mostly a glider and that it did not flap its wings very much. Others believe that it flew a lot of the time, flapping its wings strongly to travel long distances. There are **arguments** for both kinds of flight.

Was it a glider?

The *Pteranodon* had some **physical** features that **resembled** the present-day albatross. For instance, its wingspan compared to its body length was quite large. Albatrosses spend a great deal of time over the sea fishing. They use air currents to soar long distances without flapping their wings. This saves energy. *Pteranodon* may have acted in the same way and that would have made it more a glider than a flyer.

Pteranodon's breastbone was small compared to the rest of its body. This would have made its flight muscles quite small too. This may mean that it spent more time gliding than actually flying.

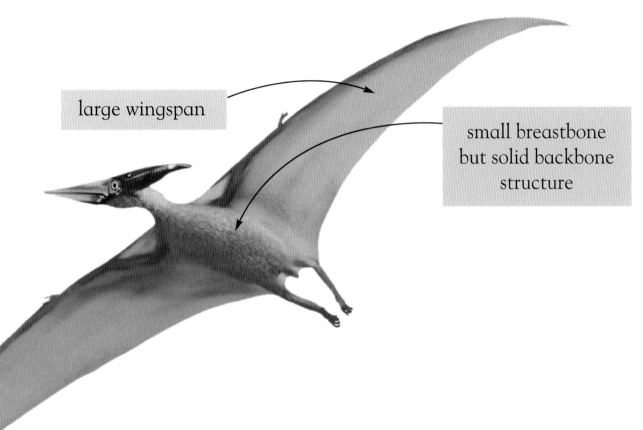

large wingspan

small breastbone but solid backbone structure

Was it a flapper?

Pteranodon's flight muscles were connected to **crests** on the bones. This could mean that it could flap its wings and use flapping power to fly. It would not have developed this ability if it had not needed to use it a lot of the time.

Its vertebrae—the bones that made up its spine—were **fused** together with its ribs to create a solid **structure**. This would have supported a good-sized flight muscle, so it probably was an excellent long-distance flapper.

Wingspan graph

All flying reptiles are called *Pterosauria*. They first took to the air during Triassic times. They continued to flourish in the Jurassic and Cretaceous periods. These **airborne** reptiles flew on wings made of skin that was stretched between a long fourth finger and the top part of their back legs. The first *Pterosaurs* had wingspans that were not that big. *Eudimorphodon's* was just 30 inches (75 centimeters) across.

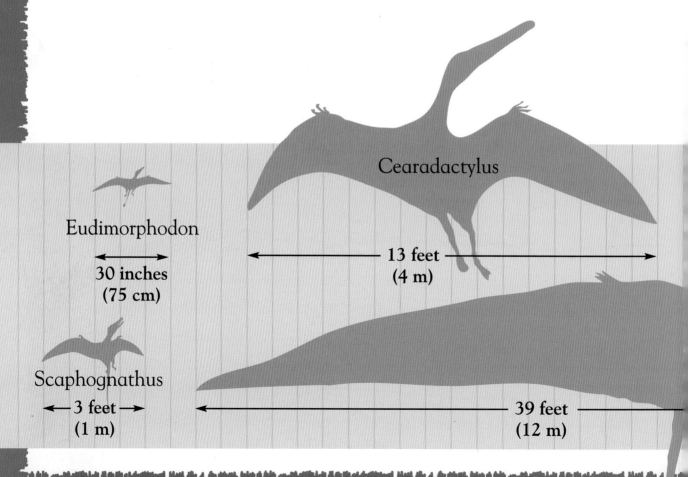

Cearadactylus

Eudimorphodon

30 inches
(75 cm)

13 feet
(4 m)

Scaphognathus

3 feet
(1 m)

39 feet
(12 m)

Different creatures wingspans grew larger and **evolved** over millions of years. *Cearadactylus* had a wingspan of 13 feet (4 meters). The last *pterosaurs* to fly had huge wingspans. Some scientists believe they were so big that it is hard to believe they could lift themselves off the ground. But somehow they did. *Quetzalcoatlus* had a wingspan of 39 feet (12 meters)—as wide as a small aircraft.

Pterosauria

Anurognathus	*12 inches (30 cm) wide*
Eudimorphodon	*30 inches (75 cm) wide*
Scaphognathus	*3 feet (1 m) wide*
Cearadactylus	*13 feet (4 m) wide*
Pteranodon	*23 feet (7 m) wide*
Quetzalcoatlus	*39 feet (12 m) wide*

Pteranodon

23 feet
(7 m)

Anurognathus

12 inches
(30 cm)

Quetzalcoatlus

Glossary

aerodynamic The ability to travel through air with the least amount of resistance

airborne Flying in the air

argument An opinion or point of view

crest Bone that sticks out from the top of the head

currents Air or water flowing in a certain direction

display To show so that others see

evolve To grow and change through time

fuse To join together

mollusks A group of animals that have a soft body and no backbone

organisms A form of life

physical Related to the body

predator An animal that hunts other animals for food

prey An animal that is hunted by another animal

resemble Having the same characteristics as, or looking like, something else

structure The parts of something that altogether form the whole thing

taper To become smaller at one end

Index

Further Reading and Websites

Pteranodon by Jinny Johnson, Smart Apple Media, 2009

Pteranodon: Giant of the Sky by David West, PowerKids Press, 2008.

Websites:

www.smithsonianeducation.org